THE
TWELVE
WILD
GEESE

Adapted and Illustrated by
MATT FAULKNER

SCHOLASTIC
HARDCOVER

SCHOLASTIC INC.
New York

Library of Congress Cataloging-in-Publication Data
Faulkner, Matt.
The twelve wild geese / written and illustrated by Matt Faulkner.   p.   cm.
Summary: Rose saves the lives of her twelve brothers after a fairy turns them into geese.
ISBN 0-590-45684-9
[1. Fairy tales. 2. Folklore—Ireland. 3. Brothers and sisters—Folklore.]   I. Title.
PZ8.F275Tw 1995
398.21—dc20   [E]   92-9709   CIP   AC

12 11 10 9 8 7 6 5 4 3 2 1   5 6 7 8 9 0/09
Printed in Singapore
First printing, March 1995   Book design by David Turner
The illustrations in this book are ink drawings over watercolor washes.

To my sweet son
Gabriel, born 8/15/91

Come away, O human child!
To the waters and the wild
With a faery, hand in hand,
For the world's more full of weeping
than you can understand.

W.B. Yeats

There once lived a king and queen who had twelve fine sons. But, alas, much to the queen's sorrow, they had not a single daughter.

One morning, while the queen sat mending the king's robes, a raven flew through the window.

The queen jumped at the bird's squawking and pricked her finger. "Aaah," sighed she. "If only I had a daughter with hair as black as the raven, cheeks as red as my blood, and skin as white as the new-fallen snow. I would trade away all my sons for such a daughter."

Suddenly, a strange little fairy woman appeared.

"Foolish one," the fairy woman chided, "that was a wicked wish. And to punish you, it shall be granted. On the day your daughter is born, you will lose each of your fine sons." So saying, the fairy departed as quickly as she had come.

The months passed and on the day the queen was to give birth, she remembered the fairy's warning. She tied her twelve sons to the bedpost with a silver silken cord. But at the very moment the queen gave birth to a daughter, each prince sprouted a pair of wings and flew over the castle walls.

Princess Rose was a beautiful child with a sunny disposition. But, as her twelfth birthday approached, Rose became quiet and gloomy. One afternoon, the queen found Rose in tears. "Child, what troubles you?" she asked.

"Oh, Mother," sobbed Rose. "It seems everyone else has a brother or a sister. I'm so lonely."

The queen sadly revealed the terrible fate that had befallen the twelve princes. "It's my fault," thought Rose. "I must rescue my brothers from their enchantment."

That night, when the moon was high, Rose left the castle. She ran all night long, stopping only when she came to a cabin nestled deep within the Wild Woods.

Rose entered the cabin. The hearth was cold and the table strewn with dirty cups and plates. Beyond lay twelve unmade beds. Too tired to care, Rose climbed into the nearest bed and fell fast asleep.

The loud flapping of wings wakened Rose from her slumber. Twelve enormous geese surrounded her.

"Who is in my bed?" cried one gander.

"Too big to be an elf," replied his brother.

"Too pretty to be a gnome," added another.

"She's a girl!" honked the eldest. "And you know how we feel about girls! I say we throw her out!"

Suddenly a strange little fairy woman appeared before them. "Put your sister down!" she cried. "Or I'll turn the lot of you into bog rats!" The geese dropped Rose at once.

"Much better," said the fairy woman. "Now listen closely, for your lives depend on it. Only Rose can free you from your enchantment. In five years, she must knit twelve sweaters, one for each of you, during which time she may neither laugh, nor cry, nor speak. If she falters but once, it's wild geese you will remain, until the end of your days!" So saying, the fairy woman vanished.

Rose set to work. She knit one sweater and then a second and a third. Three years passed. One morning an enormous wolfhound burst in on Rose. A young man rushed to her side. He apologized and said, "I am the new king of the lands to the north. May I have the pleasure of your acquaintance?"

Rose blushed a deep red but remained silent. As for the young king, it was love at first sight. He asked Rose to marry him that day.

Rose nodded eagerly, for strange as it may seem she had also fallen in love. Together, Rose and the dashing young king left the Wild Woods.

That very night, the knights and ladies of the castle celebrated the marriage of the young king and his new bride. Everyone rejoiced. Everyone, that is, except the king's stepmother. High up in her tower, the jealous old queen plotted the downfall of the beautiful new queen.

For many months the king and queen were happy together. And yet, Rose remained faithful to the promise she had made. She never spoke a word, and only set aside her knitting one year later, to give birth to a baby boy.

Everyone welcomed the new prince. Everyone, that is, except the king's stepmother. High up in her tower, the old queen plotted against the young queen and the baby prince.

On a moonless night, the wicked queen slipped a sleeping potion into Rose's goblet. When Rose fell into a deep sleep, the old queen crept into the royal bedchamber, snatched the prince, and threw him from the castle window. A great owl swooped down and caught the baby. "By all means, take him," cackled the old queen.

The next morning the old queen shed crocodile tears. "How strange that Rose does not weep for her missing child," she whispered into the king's ear. Rose was miserable, yet she would not break her vow of silence.

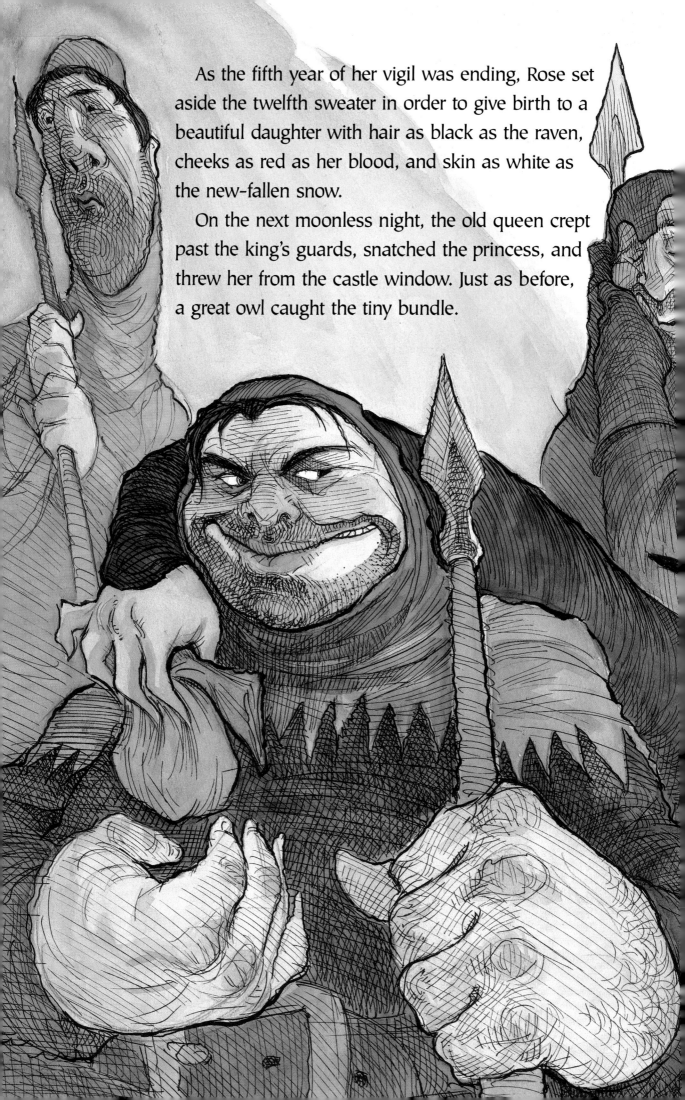

As the fifth year of her vigil was ending, Rose set aside the twelfth sweater in order to give birth to a beautiful daughter with hair as black as the raven, cheeks as red as her blood, and skin as white as the new-fallen snow.

On the next moonless night, the old queen crept past the king's guards, snatched the princess, and threw her from the castle window. Just as before, a great owl caught the tiny bundle.

The following morning, the old
queen was the first to accuse Rose.
"The Witch of the Wild Woods is
to blame!"

The king begged Rose to defend
herself, but she would not break her vow.

"Her silence proves her guilt!" cried the old queen.
"Burn the witch!"

Just as Rose was completing the last sweater, she was
seized and tied to the stake. Suddenly, there was a thunderous
clapping, as if the wings of a hundred angels were beating
back the flames.

Twelve enormous geese flew to her side. As Rose tossed
the sweaters over their slender necks, the wild geese were
transformed into her brothers. They rescued Rose at once.

Rose spoke for the first time in five years, revealing the labor of love she had taken upon herself. As the young king embraced Rose, the fairy woman appeared, carrying the royal babes. "It was I in the shape of an owl who saved the children from the wicked queen. Through much sacrifice, Queen Rose has proven herself loyal, steadfast, and true." So saying, the fairy departed before the king and queen could thank her.

"All hail Queen Rose!" The crowd sent up a cheer and the celebrations began.

As for the king's wicked stepmother, she was never heard from again. But to this day, the royal gardener complains about a noisy old crow, haunting the castle grounds.